This book belongs to...

_____

_____

_____

STINKY

Hamster Sitter Wanted

An original concept by author Tracy Gunaratnam

© Tracy Gunaratnam

Illustrations by Hannah Marks

Hannah is represented by Astound

www.astound.us

Published by MAVERICK ARTS PUBLISHING LTD

Studio 3a, City Business Centre, 6 Brighton Road,

Horsham, West Sussex, RH13 5BB +44 (0) 1403 256941

First Published in the UK in 2017 by © **MAVERICK ARTS PUBLISHING LTD**

American edition published in 2019 by Maverick Arts Publishing, distributed in
the United States and Canada by Lerner Publishing Group Inc., 241 First Avenue
North, Minneapolis, MN 55401 USA

ISBN: 978-1-84886-359-0

Maverick
publishing

www.maverickbooks.co.uk

distributed by **Lerner**

Hamster Sitter
WANTED

Written by
Tracy Gunaratnam

Illustrated by
Hannah Marks

Marco and Polo climbed into their rocket. Today they were flying to Mars...

5,
4,
3,
2...

"SURPRISE!"

cried Fudge, Smudge, Bonkers, Conkers, Nipper, Kipper, Pinky, Stinky, Crumble, Bumble and the rest.

"**Oh no**... it's my cousins," said Marco.
Fudge handed Marco an icky, sticky note.

"That's it," said Marco, "No more adventures for us."

"Nonsense," Polo replied, "What we need is a hamster sitter."

HAMSTER SITTER WANTED!

Marco and Polo made posters and leaflets and they even put an advert in the Daily Whale.

Mrs Baaton arrived
the next morning.

"Don't worry," she said,
"I've brought plenty of
wool to keep the little
dears busy."

"Thank you Mrs Baaton," said Marco,
"we'll be back this evening."
"Let's go," whispered Polo.
The two friends made a dash for the door.

Skydiving was an absolute scream.

But by the time they got home...

Poor Mrs Baaton was totally wound up.

"I won't be coming back," she bleated.

Marco marched the hamsters to bed.

Mr Yogani showed up the following morning.

"Hello hamsters," he said, "I'm looking after you today...

"...and we're going to practice **yoga**."

Marco and Polo made a quick getaway.

They climbed Mount Everest and were on top of the world.

But by the time they got home...

Poor Mr Yogani had been whirled
and twirled into a very large pretzel.

"You won't be seeing me again!" he cried.

Marco marched the hamsters to bed.

"You were right," sighed Polo.
"No more adventures for us."

The next day Marco and Polo had a garage sale.

"Good Morning," said Ms Bottomus. "I've come to hamster sit."

Marco shook his head, "Too dangerous," he said.

"Nonsense!" Ms Bottomus replied, "**Hamster sitting** is what I do best. Leave the little nippers with me."

Lion dancing was a roaring success. And when they got home...

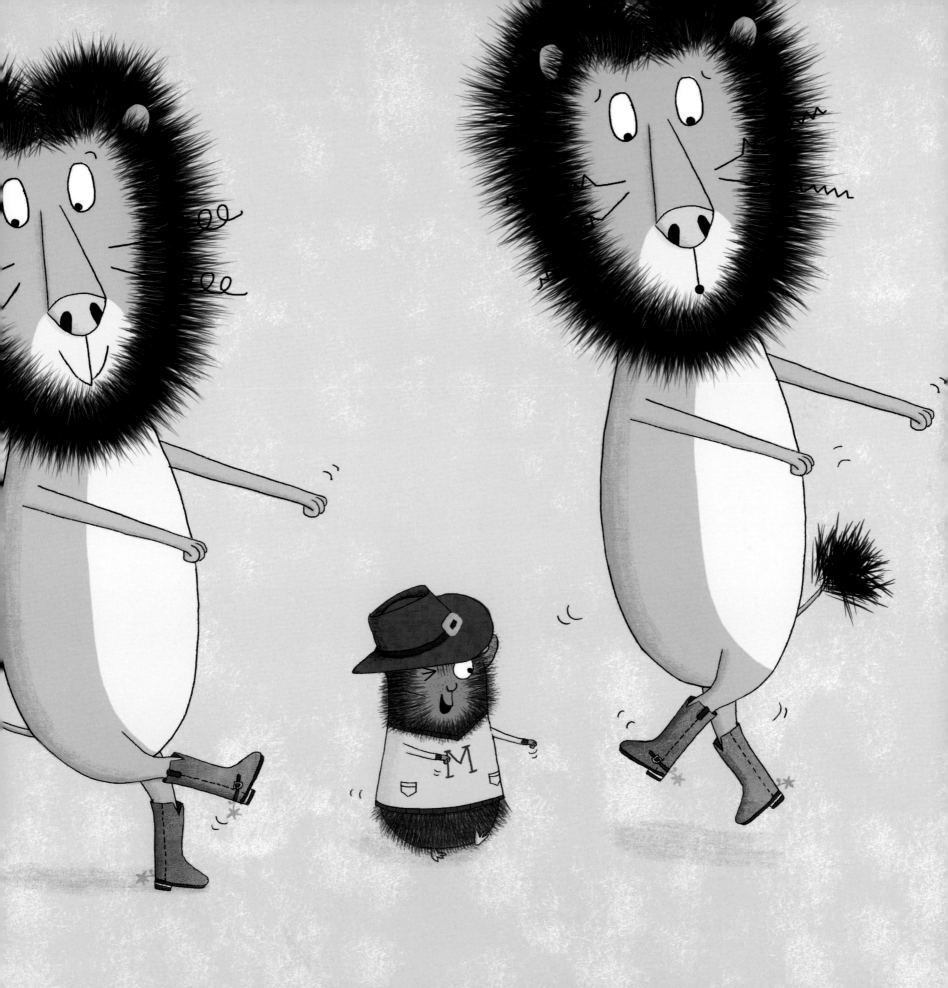

"Your hamsters have been as **good as gold**," said Ms Bottomus.

"Our troubles are finally over," sighed Marco.

"Absolutely," agreed Ms Bottomus.

"No buts about it!"

The End

Illustrator's Note:

The illustrations for this book were made digitally within Photoshop. A collage of lively patterns and textures created an organic and unique feel to this brilliant story.